P9-DBL-538

The Unruly Queen

E. S. Redmond

Candlewick Press

Thank you to Mom and Kevin for your love and support, to Eden and Griffin for your endless inspiration, and, as always, to Joan and Maryellen for your enthusiasm and insight.

First edition 2012

Library of Congress Cataloging-in-Publication Data is available.

Library of Congress Catalog Card Number 2011018607

ISBN 978-0-7636-3445-2

11 12 13 14 15 16 SCP 10 9 8 7 6 5 4 3 2 1

Printed in Humen, Dongguan, China

This book was typeset in Filosophia Regular. The illustrations were done in pen and ink and watercolor.

Candlewick Press
99 Dover Street
Somerville, Massachusetts 02144

visit us at www.candlewick.com

Minerva von Vyle was a mischievous child
who was coddled and spoiled and allowed to run wild.
She was peevish and pushy and got her own way
by throwing hysterical fits every day.

Her parents were privileged and preoccupied
with purchasing everything money could buy.
Between shopping and luncheons and weekends in Rome,
they scarcely spent time with Minerva at home.

So Minerva made mischief—she stayed up till dawn.
She rode her pink pony and tore up the lawn.
She drew on the walls with indelible ink
and insisted on sugary sodas to drink.
She jumped on the beds; she raced down the halls,
and during peak hours, made long-distance calls.

No one was spared from the havoc she wreaked.
She had fifty-two nannies in fifty-two weeks.
Each one of them left feeling frazzled and freaked,
with permanent headaches and hair with white streaks.

Just when it seemed no relief was in store,
the fifty-third nanny appeared at their door.
She'd stepped in and no sooner
set her bags down
when she heard a commotion
and loud crashing sounds.

Minerva was standing on top of her chair,
refusing to eat what the chef had prepared.
She had thrown her beef Wellington onto the floor,
insisting her dinner resembled manure.

"Now bring me a plateful of candy instead . . .
and don't even think about mentioning bed!
I also want cookies and a glass of warm milk
and my soft, pink pajamas that are made out of silk!"

The chef and the butler and both of her maids
were desperate and scrambling to stop her tirade.

But the fifty-third nanny stood frozen and smiled
and said she was honored to meet the young child
who the Order of Nannies agreed, as a whole,
is the "single most difficult child to control."

"Therefore," she went on with her eyes all agleam,
"I have come here to crown you the Unruly Queen!"

"A queen?" shrieked Minerva. "How perfect for me!
I'm practically royal, as I'm sure you can see!
I already have diamonds and a private chauffeur,
and I don't have an issue with wearing real fur!"

"Precisely, Minerva!"
The new nanny beamed.
"It appears that you'll make
an exceptional queen!"

"Now, you'll rule from
a place of which people don't speak—
it's a dark distant place known as Petulant Peak.
It's a treacherous climb up a prickly ascend
and is shrouded in darkness just beyond your Wits' End."

"Are there views from the castle? Will I sit on a throne?
Can I order room service on a solid-gold phone?"

"Even better!" the fifty-third nanny declared,
excitedly clasping her hands in the air.

"High on the mountain, underneath a black cloud,
you will live among creatures so loathsome and loud.
You will scuttle about in a dark dingy cave
and banish all beasties who dare to behave!"

"But what about dollies and pink satin sheets?
And a butler whose job is to offer me sweets?"

"Nonsense!" Nanny chirped, sounding rather amused,
while Minerva was growing more irked and confused.
"There aren't any butlers on Petulant Peak,
but there are creature comforts." She smiled. "So to speak."

"Minerva, you must simply be overjoyed
at the thought of such havoc and horrendous noise!
You can smash things to bits! Throw your food on the floor!
Nobody's going to care anymore!"

"But I'm not like that!" snapped Minerva quite loud.
"Sure, you are," Nanny said. "And you should be proud!
You can be your true self up on top of that hill.
After all, you're the Unruly Queen. Aren't you thrilled?"
Minerva clenched both of her fists by her side
and unleashed a cavernous ear-crushing cry:

"But what sort of a queen

ives with beasts in a cave?"

"The sort," Nanny answered,

"who *never* behaves."

"I behave," hissed Minerva, shaking and irate.
"Don't be silly," said Nanny. "It's terribly late.
You aren't in bed, and you can't be cajoled
into doing a singular thing that you're told."

"Can, too!" she exploded,

her cheeks burning red.

"I am going to go and get ready for bed!"

M

"Oh, I wouldn't," warned Nanny, "not if I were you.
Just think of the damage behaving could do.
You might lose your crown, and you'd surely be snubbed.
Good heavens, Minerva! Are you in the tub?"

"No, no," Nanny scoffed, "you're much too pristine.
We can't have a sweet-smelling rose for the queen!
Not to worry, my dear. We mustn't despair!
You still look a wreck with those knots in your hair."

Then Minerva defiantly picked up a brush,
and she frantically combed till her face was all flushed.
"Oh, bother," sniffed Nanny, "what a terrible pity.
You don't look like the queen should—you look far too pretty."

Minerva ignored her and marched to the sink—
she brushed her teeth twice and had water to drink.

"Oh, no," Nanny groaned, "this simply won't do.
You've put on pajamas and brushed your teeth, too!
Are you planning to keep on behaving this way?
And risk throwing the chance of a lifetime away?"

Minerva looked at her pile of porcelain dolls,
her huge feather bed and her hand-painted walls.
She thought of the butler, the chef, and the maids—
how they always brought sweets and fresh pink lemonade.
Then she thought about life up on Petulant Peak,
and her future felt suddenly dreary and bleak.

"I'm going to keep on behaving," she said,
and she lifted the unruly crown from her head.

"Oh, well," sighed the nanny, sounding sad and serene,
"I'm afraid if you do, then you cannot be queen.
Seems a pity, Minerva," the nanny kept on.
"Sometimes we don't know what we've got till it's gone."

"I suppose we *could* crown a replacement instead."
And she turned out the light that was next to the bed.
Then she paused before finally closing the door,
turning back toward Minerva to say one thing more:

"But, of course, I must stay to make certain, my dear—
you should know that we crown a new queen every year."